A NOTE TO PARENTS

When your children are ready to "step into reading," giving them the right books is as crucial as giving them the right food to eat. **Step into Reading Books** present exciting stories and information reinforced with lively, colorful illustrations that make learning to read fun, satisfying, and worthwhile. They are priced so that acquiring an entire library of them is affordable. And they are beginning readers with a difference—they're written on five levels.

Early Step into Reading Books are designed for brand-new readers, with large type and only one or two lines of very simple text per page. **Step 1 Books** feature the same easy-to-read type as the Early Step into Reading Books, but with more words per page. **Step 2 Books** are both longer and slightly more difficult, while **Step 3 Books** introduce readers to paragraphs and fully developed plot lines. **Step 4 Books** offer exciting nonfiction for the increasingly independent reader.

The grade levels assigned to the five steps—preschool through kindergarten for the Early Books, preschool through grade 1 for Step 1, grades 1 through 3 for Step 2, grades 2 through 3 for Step 3, and grades 2 through 4 for Step 4—are intended only as guides. Some children move through all five steps very rapidly; others climb the steps over a period of several years. Either way, these books will help your child "step into reading" in style!

http://www.randomhouse.com/

Library of Congress Cataloging-in-Publication Data:
Coxe, Molly. R is for radish / by Molly Coxe.   p.   cm. — (Step into reading: A Step 2 book)
SUMMARY: Radish the rabbit has adventures at school, finding a way to learn her spelling
words, discovering fun at recess, and more.
ISBN 0-679-88574-9 (pbk.) — ISBN 0-679-98574-3 (lib. bdg.)
[1. Rabbits—Fiction. 2. Schools—Fiction.] I. Title. II. Series. PZ7.C839424Re 1997
[E]—dc21 97-10046

Printed in the United States of America   10 9 8 7 6 5 4 3 2 1

STEP INTO READING is a registered trademark of Random House, Inc.

Step into Reading®

R is for Radish!

by Molly Coxe

A Step 2 Book

Random House New York

1

R-a-p

Radish was writing
her spelling words.
Mrs. Mink said,
"Tomorrow we will have
a spelling bee."

"Y–U–C–K," wrote Radish.
"The winner will get
a banana split,"
Mrs. Mink said.
"Y–U–M!" wrote Radish.

That night after dinner,
Radish took out the spelling list.
She wrote "glue" and "junk"
four times each.
"This is B–O–R–I–N–G,"
thought Radish.

junk
junk
junk
junk

Radish hopped downstairs
to the basement.
Her big sister Roz
was listening to rap.

Radish put on a pair
of sunglasses.
"G–L–U–E,
it sticks to you,
it sticks to me.
J–U–N–K,
the stuff you have to
throw away,"
rapped Radish.

Radish rapped spelling words
until bedtime.

The next morning,

she lined up

for the spelling bee.

"Snail," said Mrs. Mink.

"Snail," said Radish.

Then her mind went blank.

"Next," said Mrs. Mink.

"Wait!" cried Radish.

She put on

her sunglasses.

She rapped,

"S–N–A–I–L,

a slimy thing

inside a shell."

After that,

Radish rapped

all her spelling words.

And the banana split

was Y–U–M–M–Y.

2

Recess

The bell rang for recess.

"I hate recess," said Radish.

"Recess is too long."

"Have you tried hopscotch?"
asked Mrs. Mink.
"My feet are too big,"
said Radish.

"How about tetherball?"

Mrs. Mink asked.

"My ears are too long,"

said Radish.

"The slide?"
asked Mrs. Mink.
"My fur is too slippery,"
said Radish.

A big ball rolled toward Radish.

"Look out!" cried Mrs. Mink.

Radish hopped high in the air.

"Aha!" said Mrs. Mink.

Mrs. Mink
found a jump rope
and started to jump.
She sang,
"Raspberry, blueberry,
pumpkin pie.
Apples, pears, gummy bears
hop so high."
"I bet I can hop higher,"
said Radish.
"I bet you can, too,"
said Mrs. Mink.

Radish was still jumping rope
when the bell rang.
"Radish, recess is over,"
shouted Mrs. Mink.

"Recess is too short,"
said Radish.

3

Rainbow

Radish wrote a play.

She called it *The Rainbow*.

"Can I be in it?"

asked her friend Pinky.

"No," said Radish.

"You'll hog the show."

"I'll let you use my sparkle markers,"
 said Pinky.

"No way," said Radish.

"And my glow-in-the-dark paints,"
 said Pinky.

"Oh, all right," said Radish.

The next day, Mrs. Mink said,

"Radish and Pinky

will now perform

Radish's new play."

Thunder crashed.

Lightning flashed.

Rain fell.

Then the sun shone,
and a rainbow appeared.

The rainbow danced.

And danced.

"That's enough,"

whispered Radish.

The rainbow kept dancing.

"Pinky, I'm warning you,"

Radish whispered.

Suddenly, there was

a crash of thunder.

Down came the rain,

and washed the rainbow

right off the stage.

"Oops," said Pinky.

"I guess I got carried away."

"You always do,"
said Radish.

"You're a ham."

"Girls, come out

and take a bow,"

said Mrs. Mink.

"You mean they *liked* it?"

said Radish.

"They loved it!" said Mrs. Mink.

"OH!" said Radish and Pinky.

Then Radish took Pinky's hand
and they stepped onto the stage.

4

Raspberry Pie

It was summer.

Radish's mother was baking
a raspberry pie.

"Is it done?" asked Radish.

"Not yet," said Mrs. Rabbit.

Radish ran outside.

Her friends were playing

flashlight tag.

"Radish is it!" cried Kat.

Radish counted to ten.

"Ready or not,

here I come!" she shouted.

Radish searched

behind the berry bushes,

on top of the woodpile,

and inside the tool shed.

But her friends

were not hiding

in any of those places.

Radish pricked up her ears.

She did not hear

her friends' voices.

Radish sniffed the air.

She did not smell

her friends' smells.

But she did smell something.

Raspberry pie!

"If I can smell it,

they can, too,"

thought Radish.

Radish hid behind a tree.
After a few minutes,
she heard footsteps.
Radish shined the flashlight
on her friend Kat.
"Got you!" said Radish.

Radish heard more footsteps.

"And you!

And you!" said Radish.

"What is that delicious smell?"
asked Freddy.

"Raspberry pie," said Radish.

"Want some?"

"Yes!" said Freddy.

"Me, too!"

"Me, too!" said the others.

"Raspberry pie,

here we come!" shouted Radish.

And that was the end
of flashlight tag.

And the end of the
raspberry pie.